Musings under the Moon

Aarushi Kulkarni

Ukiyoto Publishing

All global publishing rights are held by

Ukiyoto Publishing

Published in 2023

Content Copyright ©Aarushi Kulkarni

ISBN 9789360498641

All rights reserved.

No part of this publication may be reproduced, transmitted, or stored in a retrieval system, in any form by any means, electronic, mechanical, photocopying, recording or otherwise, without the prior permission of the publisher.

The moral rights of the author have been asserted.

This is a work of fiction. Names, characters, businesses, places, events, locales, and incidents are either the products of the author's imagination or used in a fictitious manner. Any resemblance to actual persons, living or dead, or actual events is purely coincidental.

This book is sold subject to the condition that it shall not by way of trade or otherwise, be lent, resold, hired out or otherwise circulated, without the publisher's prior consent, in any form of binding or cover other than that in which it is published.

www.ukiyoto.com

Dedication

This book is dedicated to all my loved ones. For their assistance, encouragement, and unwavering support, I would like to thank my mother, my grandparents, my aunt Madhavi Murthy, and my grandaunt Sudha Gorthi.

Acknowledgement

I would also like to thank my best friends- Diipit, Arohi, Samanvi, and Sahitya. Your unwavering support and belief in me has helped me improve my writing skills and has made this book possible. Lastly, I would like to thank my cousin - Anindita for the lovely illustrations.

Contents

Comfort	1
The Big Beyond	2
Sainikpuri, Secunderabad	3
What Makes Me Happy?	4
Monsoon Afternoon	5
Memories	6
Growing Up	7
Realisations	8
Brando	9
Amma	10
Baba	11
Nature's Painting	12
The Ocean	13
Regret	14
Joys of School Days	**Error! Bookmark not defined.**
The Party	16
Memories Of Baba	17
A House I Can Call Home	18
The Mourning Mother's Cry	19
Happiness	21
Sadness	22
5th September	23
The Countryside	25
The Evenings Of Autumn	26
Spring Day	27
A Reunion	28
Family	29
Grandpa	30

A Night Spent Right	31
The Pain I Wrote About	32
`This Is For The Better`	33
Insecurities	34
Pain And Comfort	35
Change	36
Healing	37
Heartbreak	38
Things That Remind Me Of Him	39
Alma Mater	40
Flowers And Scars	41
An Army Veteran	42
About the Author	*44*

Comfort

When I was a kid, I was told a story,
About an angel who brought me where I now call home
Sometimes I wish that angel could come back
Just wave her wand and fix everything
Solve all the puzzles of life
To tell me not to give up
To comfort me
Give me a warm hug when I am on the edge
To say that those insecurities are nothing
To teach me to love myself, live my life
To give me hope and happiness
Where is this angel, I wondered?
Until someone told me that
This angel lives within us, and we just need to seek her.

*****

The Big Beyond

The sky intrigues me the most...
You can't touch the sky, yet it is the limit.
The clouds float in the sky, which is always behind them.

I had written a story about the clouds...
How they gain their beautiful colours when the sun sets and rises –
The daughter of the Sun God walks on the clouds,
Wearing a beautiful rainbow gown which gives it the colours we see...

The sun is the brightest and biggest and hottest
But hides behind mountains, buildings, trees and clouds
The moon is the only companion …..

The moon is always around... never rises and never sets.
It brings along stars and light to guide us through

The stars are small but also are the only ones that twinkle...
They move around in the night sky, forming shapes that we can gaze upon.
They say stars are the departed loved ones that shine for us.
Looking at them gives me peace and courage.

*****

Sainikpuri, Secunderabad

The warm breeze blowing on a peaceful winter afternoon
In this little part of a big city
A town, you could call it,
A world of its own.
Houses beautifully built and coated with delicate colours.
Small gardens surrounding them,
With huge trees, small plants and creepers engulfing the walls
And a gate at which the dogs laze around.
Birds singing in a choir.
The gentle sound of the silence as the town relaxes
Just like me, sitting up in my room, near the window
And reading a book about another magical place just like this.

****

What Makes Me Happy?

She smiled through her clouded eyes
Like the sun shining through the dark clouds.
Tears rolled down her cheeks
Like the rain drops down the window-pane.
A rainbow formed as her smile widened through her tears
As she thought of the little things that brought her happiness-
The sight of a flower blooming,
The sound of the rain falling,
The smell of new books,
The taste of homemade food,
The love that felt like home.

*****

Monsoon Afternoon

In the corner of the room, I sat on a cosy chair

Reading a murder mystery.

I looked up to discover little drops of water creating ripples on the pool.

It was drizzling.

I poured my cup of tea quick enough to see the rain.

I sat on the swing, the smell of rain mixing in the cool wind that blew.

Rain, cool breeze, a cup of tea, a good book and me on the swing - a perfect afternoon!

*****

Memories

Memories get the best of us
They can make us cry, smile, or laugh when we are sad.
Some memories are so precious that we keep them locked away
And never open the treasure-chest
Some are always on our mind, never forgotten,
Maybe they aren't meant to be forgotten,
Maybe they are there to teach you a lesson or to teach you that
Some memories that are sad can be turned into happy ones...
You don't need to be at a place or do something for your
 Memories to resurface, as long as they're in your heart.

****

Growing Up

The sparkling water creating ripples in the puddles.
The rain drops glistening on lily pads,
Falling off the blades of grass.
As I looked down upon the pristine scenery,
Remembering the rainy days of ten years ago.
A long way we all have come
From loving to hating it.

We were kids back then,
Kids who made paper boats for the puddles,
Kids who danced in the rain,
Kids who weren't afraid of getting drenched,
Kids who let their tears mix with the rain,
Kids who let rainbows form on their faces,
Kids who never hid from the rain.

Now we fear the rain,
Fear the soaking of our clothes
Fear soggy shoes
Fear the wetting of the papers-
Fear all the adult things
Oh! How I wish we could go back to the carefree days!

****

Realisations

I sat at the window-sill with my dairy,
Reminiscing events from my childhood.
I am glad that I took notes of my life back then
Because it made me realise that
We have changed so much.
We aren't those little kids anymore.
We aren't excited for trivial nor vital things.
We cry a lot but laugh little.
We are so into our life and its problems that we have forgotten
Who we are.
Today, I am hurt at how change came in like the wind
And how the stormy clouds took over the bright sunny sky.

****

Brando

I was standing there with cute puppies jumping around me
But my eyes were fixed on this one puppy -
Under the shelf he lay,
Hiding away because he was shy.
I chose him-
Not because he was the youngest or the cutest (which he was)
But chose him because he was the odd one out, shy,
Afraid to come out, scared to trust someone
I chose him because he was like me.
He is eight now and is rough and tough
At the same time delicate and wispy,
My brother – "Brando".

*****

Amma

Her gentle hands moved the curtains
To witness the blissful scene.
The sun drowning in the ocean of clouds,
The wind playing with the trees,
The leaves falling to make a layer on the grass.
A moment of silence and everything faded
As a tear rolled down her soft pink cheeks,
Pushing her back into the darkness she was in.

****

Baba

I stood there, in the middle of the busy footpath,
Watching him walk into the crowd of people.
I knew that there was no point in standing there,
But my heart said, "He'll come back... Just wait..."
And I did - but he didn't return.
I saw the sun sink into the horizon
And the moon floating in the air, but he didn't return.
It was time; nature said so, time to move on from everything
Leaving it where I was standing and to move forward
One step at a time, one foot forward at a time.

*****

Nature's Painting

The cold frothy water playing kabbadi with my feet
The warm sand running through my fingers
The sound of the waves ringing in my ears
The pretty sight of children collecting shells…
It was a painting before me
The sun drowning through the ocean of clouds,
Touching the edge of the sky and water
And slowly landing on the waves
The definition of peace in one scenery.

*****

The Ocean

The small and the big live in the ocean
The sun and the moon reflect upon the glistening water
The ocean has moods of its own
At times it can be raging with anger
At times it can be as calm as the sand on the shore.
It looks never ending but -
Brings shells to little girls, frothy water to the ankles,
Peace to the heart.
The sun drowns through the ocean of clouds,
Touching the edge of the sky and water,
slowly landing on the waves.

*****

Regret

A lot of times we want to say things to certain people
We want to go up to them and say sorry
Go up to them and get re-acquainted.
Unless we are the lucky ones,
We don't get to say what's in our hearts, and with time
We flow like the river, making our own path
Moving on like the other people in our life,
who blow in and out like the wind.

" Kabhi kabhi aditi zindagi mein yuhin koi apna lagta hain
Kabhi kabhi aditi woh bichad jaye to ek sapna lagta hain..."

*****

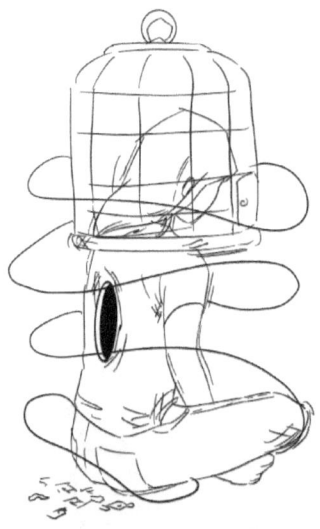

Joys of School Days

Running in the corridors, getting caught
In the lunch break, winning those pen fights that we fought
Going to the washroom, just to scare and prank
Climbing four flights of stairs, sweating and tired
But with a bundle of jokes to crack
Oh! Such fun we had in school with friends by our side!

Laughing at the lamest jokes
Teachers scolding me and my folks
Talking more, eating less
On our tables we created a mess
Those bus rides, those roasts, those stories…
Ah! Our school days are fun with friends by our side.

*****

The Party

Glasses clicking,
'Cheers' being exclaimed,
Laughter everywhere.
Bottles standing,
Snacks passed around,
Sitting under the starry sky.
The perfect night
With perfect people.

*****

Memories Of Baba

The twinkle in your eyes,
Makes my heart shine so bright,
Those laughing lips,
Make me smile,
Those dark eyes staring at me,
Remind me of a grey sky full of clouds,
Yet they show the warmth of your smile.
Sun setting, wind blowing,
Sitting in the balcony with you
Music playing, talking, laughing
These are the strings of joy
Made right here at home.

*****

A House I Can Call Home

As I opened the gate, Dougie the dog ran up to me.
Moving forward after petting her, I entered the house.
The aromatic smell of the food drifted through the air,
A melodious song played on the radio.
I moved further inside and come across a gorgeous painting of pink lotuses.
As I walked towards the spiral staircase,
The groaning of the swing echoed,
On which I saw a little girl
Reading her book and swinging.
The book belonged to the library adjacent to the swing,
Which I visited on my way back from the courtyard.

I glanced into the room with the view of the cool pool
 Upon which the sunlight gently swayed.
I made my way up the stairs and into the red room,
Then the blue room, white room,
And lastly the yellow room.
The blue room had a door, not a magical one alas –
 As I opened the door, I saw grass under the hammock
 And the sun hiding behind the trees
And the breeze played with my hair.
 Sad to say that the tour of this magical abode ends here,
 But happy to say that it belongs to a wonderful family
- My family.

The Mourning Mother's Cry

My eyes are clouded just like the sky,
My tears are falling like the rain,
The thunder can be heard for miles,
But like always, stifled are my cries
Because it is I … that must always pay the price.

What is happening to this world?
Trees ruthlessly slaughtered for timber,
Baby animals crying for their mothers' dead.
A sunless sky choking with smog,
The dying sighs of the lake and bog,
The green struggling amongst the grey.
Should our planet be this way?

What is happening to the world?
No animal is free,
Not a leaf on a tree.
Garbage here,
Plastic there.
Hot in the summer,
Hot in the winter,
The Earth is boiling with anger!

The greed of your species knows no bounds,
Sundering the bonds delicately woven

With nature, with the soul, with the animals,
With Me, Mother Earth myself!

It has taken a virus to lock you in
And set free the nature,
Is this not enough to make you
Fear for your future?
How much do you really need?
And how endless is your greed?!

Wake up people! Wake up!
Wake up and look-
Mend the bonds,
Help our angry dying Earth,
Let nature revive its colours,
Let me show my happiness,
Let me live my days everlasting.

Stand up for the planet!
And, once again-
The birds line up on your balcony,
Animals roam free,
The trees dance in the wind,
The weather pleasant as can be-
This is the Earth that should be,
This is the commitment that must be
And if you abide,
 It shall be the Earth we all wish it to be.

Happiness

The people around her, laughing and smiling
The light breeze playing with her hair
The moon rising alongside the cloudy sunset
The pink hue of the horizon,
And her beloved cycle.

These were the little things
That drew a smile on her face.

*****

Sadness

Puddles of water on the ground,
And even bigger are the ones in my heart.
The leaves on trees have drops of water,
While tears are on my eyelashes.
Outside is where no one goes,
My heart is where no one is.

It's raining outside
While I am drowning inside.

*****

5th September

They forget their specs, but not their vision
They forget their books, but not their wisdom
Often weaving their own experiences to show us the road ahead
Warn us about the difficulties, wanting nothing in return
Teaching us lessons far beyond those in school
Who else would do all this for us?

They make our classes fun just so we don't sleep.
They forget to eat, to rest, just for us ….
Who are these people who do so much for us?

They help us when we have problems,
Encourage us is what they do
They don't care about our position in society
Or where we are from
They forget who they scolded
They may forget many things -
But one thing they never forget – their students!
Who are these people who care so much about us?

Teachers - they are known as
They love us like their own
They are our second parents-
Gods on Earth for us kids

Even though we are aware of this-
When do we pause to thank?

Today is the day to express our heart-felt gratitude-
GururBrahma GururVishnu GururDevo Maheshwaraha
Gurur Saakshaat ParaBrahma Tasmai Sri Gurave Namaha!!

*****

The Countryside

Wandering the roads,
All alone in the dark.
Stumbling upon a meadow,
Carpeted in green.
Staring at the fireflies,
That look like stars in the night sky.

*****

The Evenings Of Autumn

The lights on the silent roads
Twinkling like stars on a clear night sky.
Empty roads like a sky with no moon.
Peeping through the clouds,
I see the sun,
Its warmth caressing my face
Like a mother with her child.
It was as blissful as could be.

*****

Spring Day

A sloping meadow adorned with an assortment of flowers.

The rolling hills carpeted with green surrounding them.

A huge tree, as old as time, stood strong at one end

Underneath which stood handsome horses.

A charcoal horse lay beneath the branches,

A chocolate horse grazed upon the velvety grass,

An ivory horse gazed fondly at his brethren

As if they were one of his kind.

Nature dimmed the lights as the sun lay upon the horizon.

The sky was painted red and orange. The clouds draped in a lovely shade of pink.

A light stroke of the moon and drops of stars slowly covered the sky.

*****

A Reunion

The jazz band playing on the patio
The lanterns hanging on trees
Young couples dancing on the grass
The cool summer breeze blowing
The hot and tasty food on the tables
The moon shining down
The stars blinking on
The three women sit at the table
A drink in hand, with beautiful dresses and trinklets
Their hair salt and pepper but
Eternally young at heart
Time slowed them down but
Their smiles shone bright
Reminiscing their childhood.

*****

Family

I realised family doesn't have to be blood relations,
when I sat with them laughing and having the best time of my life.
My smile had gone for a long winter vacation
 but now it's back as flowers blossom in my heart again.
I could call them my life saviours because
they brought happiness into my dark world.
They picked up pieces of my heart and joined them with their love.
You can call it fate, destiny, luck, whatever-
but when I am with them all I ever think of is - Home sweet Home.

*****

Grandpa

With silver hair
And a soft gaze
He sat on the rocking chair.
With glasses on the bridge of his nose,
A book in his tender hands,
He sang away to glory.
A glass of rum
And wisdom in his words
He sat there reciting his memories.
A golden heart he had
With a few things to say
But each word of his held
comfort, love and advice.
Who else could this man be
With a charming smile and
A knowledge of years?
None other than my Grandpa.

*****

A Night Spent Right

I lay in comfort of my love, my bed
Hugging my pillows like I won't leave them
Even if the world is ending
Staring out of my window
At the leaves that make lovely prints against the blue sky in the day
And at night, how the stars shine bright against the black ocean.

*****

The Pain I Wrote About

Tears fell staining the paper with a beautiful ink painting
The tears fell but I didn't stop writing
I couldn't say anything, so I was determined to write it.
Penning each word, pouring my heart out,
I wrote everything I wished I had said back then.
There wasn't regret or guilt of not saying it
But now a wish, a wish to talk.

*****

`This Is For The Better`

To dear best friend,
From talking 24/7 to nodding at each other.
Some laughs to silence.
From stares to indifference.
From best friends to acquaintances.
Who have we became?
What are we?
What happened?
You stopped caring.
You never thought about us.
But alas we were just kids then,
Cause now I have vanished from your life
Just leaving my ashes behind,
Wishing you a happy life
~From: Aarushi

*****

Insecurities

You thought I wouldn't notice?
How you cover your eyes to hide your tears.
How you hide your smile because you think it's ugly.
How you stifle your sobs to not burden someone.
How you laugh very little because you're embarrassed.
Hiding in the shadows so no one can see you.
Well I do notice and let me tell you one thing:
When you cry, you aren't weak
When you smile, you are the most beautiful
When you share your pain, you gain a friend
When you laugh, you are happy
When you come out from behind the clouds,
 You realise that you are the sun
So no matter what happens and who you are
Always love yourself and be yourself.

*****

Pain And Comfort

I heard the glass shattering as I entered the house.
I ran to the direction of the sound
To witness a heart wrenching scene in the balcony.
She sat in the middle of the broken glass pieces,
Leaning on to the parapet of the balcony,
Tears flowing down with no signs of stopping,
In need of all the love and care, she sat there sobbing...

I was sitting in the balcony,
Thinking about my past when tears trickled down my cheeks.
The next thing I knew, the glass in my hand fell and
I had a breakdown.
While the tears kept flowing, I got breathless,
My heart was racing and I was gulping air.
In my middle tying a knot,
I felt two arms engulfing me.
I immediately felt the warmth of the body and the loving words.
To the person I saw when I calmed down: Thankyou!
I will love you always and you will remain in my heart forever.

*****

Change

I sat in the same place,
Staring into nothingness
As my mind reeled back to old memories.
The same place,
But they were not there.
The same place
But the laughter had died down.
The same place
But the talking turned to whispering walls.
The same place
But this time it was just me.

*****

Healing

Looking at the corner
Watching the memories reel back in
I wish that I could cast a spell
To bring him back for a day,
To say I am sorry
To say I love you
To say that I wish I could have helped you

Even though he is in a better place than this world,
He has left behind memories,
Scars and broken hearts.

From crying to smiling while remembering him,
I grew up.

*****

Heartbreak

The glass slipped from my hand

And shattered,

I was bleeding

But no on came.

It all felt familiar

Maybe it was deja vu

Cause I know my heart broke the same way.

*****

Things That Remind Me Of Him

I was covering my notebooks today and I remembered how I would sit on the table and my dad would cut the paper and fold them to cover the books.

Everytime I tighten a screw or change the battery it reminds me of him.

Everytime I eat varan (dal in Maharashtrian style) or dahi with salt and pepper it reminds me of him.

Alas the skies don't take calls for help or else I would have asked him to come down to help me cover my damn notebooks (cause mujhse toh nahi ho Raha Bhai).

*****

Alma Mater

Looking back at the building which
Housed our secrets forever so long,
Had our memories etched in it's walls,
Captured our laughs and cries in its corridors-
It was a treasure chest of our times there,
Everything we went through alone and together
Taking the pearls in our hearts
We walked out the gates together,
Just as we had walked in-
With sad smiles and hopes of coming back.

*****

Flowers And Scars

I have always wanted
To draw flowers on her hand.
I wanted to grow a garden of life
On the scars she made to be lifeless.
I wanted to make a bouquet of wild flowers
To show her how beautiful she is;
To show her that she could be wild and free,
That she could be herself.
I wanted to tell her that life is an
Assortment of flowers,
Of all colors, shapes and sizes.
You can't tell which flower comes from which garden
But they all have a story to tell.

*****

An Army Veteran

When I look back to the times we spent, I vividly remember
Seeing his eyes shine bright when he spoke of his army days,
A glint of mischief when he would crack a joke and
 How he fondly called his granddaughters pichipullamma!
I knew him for a short time of 16 years
And each time we met, I left with a box of memories and stories.
One such memory was when I was giving him his birthday gift,
And he asked me to do the army salute before he received it.

I never got a chance to see him in uniform-
An olive green, neatly pressed uniform
Or the judge's long black coat-
And I don't regret this
Because when seated at the Indo-Pak border,
Watching the processions,
I could let my imagination run free.

*****

Anjaane anjaane mein galti kar dete hain
Toh dil, bin bole maaf kar deta hain
Agar vahi galti dauraye jaye toh
Dil hain ki manta nahi.

*****

Kayi cheezein jane dete hain
Par use nahi
Kayi cheezein jane dete hain
Par use nahi
Uske yaadein pakadke rakhna chahte hain
Par voh ghum ko nahi.

Kash voh rehe jate humesha ke liye
Humare aakhon ke samne
Humare bahon mein
Humare dil ke paas.

*****

Ghar se bhag kar aeroplane dekhna
Pani mein paper boat chalana
Rainbow ko dekh kar uchchalna
Pani ke boondon ke neeche nachna
Yahi hain baarish ki choti si kushiyaan

About the Author

Aarushi Kulkarni

Aarushi Kulkarni is a 16-year-old student who loves to dance, read write and occasionally dabbles in baking. Aarushi is an aspiring lawyer who also plans on starting an NGO in the future. What initially started as a writing competition, helped her discover her love for writing, especially poetry. She took to writing to express her feelings when words couldn't. She writes about emotions, people and memories associated with them. With this book, Musings under the Moon, she wants to express her feelings, thoughts and experiences of the past few years and hopes that her readers find themselves in these pages and feel seen.

www.ingramcontent.com/pod-product-compliance
Lightning Source LLC
LaVergne TN
LVHW041637070526
838199LV00052B/3414